For Déirdre

This edition published in 1999 by Diamond Books
77-85 Fulham Palace Road,
Hammersmith, London, W6 8JB

First published in Great Britain by Orchard Books 1988
First published in Picture Lions 1990

Picture Lions is an imprint of the Children's Division, part of
HarperCollins Publishers Limited,
77-85 Fulham Palace Road, Hammersmith
London W6 8JB

Copyright © 1988 by Siobhan Dodds

ISBN 0 261 67378 5

Printed and bound in Singapore by Tien Wah Press

Sarah Bulldog

Siobhan Dodds

It was another morning.
Sarah Bulldog yawned and
pricked up her ears.

tweet-tweet chirped the birds

tick-tock ticked the clock

waa waa cried the baby

rattle rattle went the toy

hush–hush said the mother

meow meow purred the cat

plip-plop dripped the tap

clatter clatter went the dishes

thud thud went the cupboard

yum-yum went Sarah Bulldog.

Breakfast time.